Dear Parent:
Your child's love of reading starts here!

Every child learns to read in a different way and at his or her own speed. You can help your young reader improve and become more confident by encouraging his or her own interests and abilities. You can also guide your child's spiritual development by reading stories with biblical values and Bible stories, like I Can Read! books published by Zonderkidz. From books your child reads with you to the first books he or she reads alone, there are I Can Read! books for every stage of reading:

SHARED READING
Basic language, word repetition, and whimsical illustrations, ideal for sharing with your emergent reader.

BEGINNING READING
Short sentences, familiar words, and simple concepts for children eager to read on their own.

READING WITH HELP
Engaging stories, longer sentences, and language play for developing readers.

READING ALONE
Complex plots, challenging vocabulary, and high-interest topics for the independent reader.

ADVANCED READING
Short paragraphs, chapters, and exciting themes for the perfect bridge to chapter books.

I Can Read! books have introduced children to the joy of reading since 1957. Featuring award-winning authors and illustrators and a fabulous cast of beloved characters, I Can Read! books set the standard for beginning readers.

A lifetime of discovery begins with the magical words "I Can Read!"

Visit www.icanread.com for information on enriching your child's reading experience.
Visit www.zonderkidz.com for more Zonderkidz I Can Read! titles.

"Man looks at how someone appears on the outside.
But I [God] look at what is in the heart."
—*1 Samuel 16:7*

ZONDERKIDZ

Little David's Big Heart
Text copyright © 2010 by Crystal Bowman
Illustrations copyright © 2010 by Frank Endersby

Requests for information should be addressed to:
Zonderkidz, *Grand Rapids, Michigan* 49530

Library of Congress Cataloging-in-Publication Data

Bowman, Crystal.
    Little David's big heart / by Crystal Bowman ; illustrated by Frank Endersby.
        p. cm. — (I can read. Level 1) (David series)
    ISBN 978-0-310-71708-9 (softcover)
    [1. Kings, queens, rulers, etc.—Fiction. 2. David, King of Israel—Fiction. 3. Conduct of life—
Fiction. 4. Christian life—Fiction. 5. Mice—Fiction.] I. Endersby, Frank, ill. II. Title.
    PZ7.B68335Lip 2010
    [E]—dc22   2008008372

Editor: Mary Hassinger
Art direction: Jody Langley

Printed in China

10 11 12 13 14 15 /SCC/ 6 5 4 3 2 1

 ZONDERkidz

I Can Read!

BEGINNING 1 READING

Little David's Big Heart

story by Crystal Bowman

pictures by Frank Endersby

Little David walked through a field.

He saw a hungry bird with a worm.

David was hungry too.

But David didn't eat worms.

"I want some cheese," said David.

David ran home

through the tall grass.

He ran faster and faster.

David ran into his yard.

Someone was talking to his father.

"Sam is here," said David's father.

"He has some good news for you."

"Someday you will be the king,"
said Sam.

"Why me?" asked little David.

"I am the smallest mouse."

"God sees your heart," said Sam.

"That is why he picked you."

Sam put his hand on David's head.

"God will be with you," he said.

David's brothers heard this.

"How can this be?" they said.

One brother said,

"He's the little brother.

Why should David be the king?"

But David was a kind brother.

He opened the icebox.

He found a big piece of cheese.

He cut it into eight pieces.

One piece was for him.

He gave the rest to his brothers.

Knock! Knock! Knock!

Someone was at the door.

David peeked out the window.

"Help us!" cried David's friends.

David opened the door.

Matt and Pat ran inside.

"A big fox came," said Matt.

"He smashed our house down."

"He wants to eat us up!" said Pat.

"Don't worry," said David.

"You may stay here.

We will ask God to help us."

The next day, David went outside.

He saw the big fox by a tree.

Little David hid under a bush.

Then David roared in a very loud voice,

"Roar! Roar! Roar!"

The fox thought it was a big bear.

He was afraid and ran far away.

Everyone talked about David.

"He is so kind," one mouse said.

"He is very brave!" said another.

The king heard about David too.

"David is going to be king,"

said the king's helper.

The king did not like this one bit!

"I know what to do," said the king.

"I'll have a party just for me!"

He asked all the mice to his party.

But he did not invite David.

"Please take this gift to the king,"
little David told his brothers.

"Why are you giving him a gift?"
asked brother Ben.

"Because he is the king," said David.

Everyone went to the king's party,
but not David.

"Here is a gift from David,"

Ben said to the king.

The king opened the gift.

It was a shiny gold coin.

"Bring David here," said the king.

The king's helper

came back with David.

"You may be little," said the king,

"but you have a big heart."

He put his arm around David.

"Someday you will be a good king."

David was glad that the king

was not mad anymore.

Years later, David became the king.

And God helped David

be a good king.